A Dangerous Encounter in the Dark...

Laura bent down over the black hole. In the distance she could hear a mighty roar.

"This must be the sound we heard," she said. "I'll bet the stream leads to the waterfall."

Hotshoe and Annie weren't listening. They were busy trying Wild Bill's cellular car phone.

It didn't work.

"We'll have to go back outside to make a call," said Hotshoe. "We had better hurry so we can meet the police when they arrive. Without our help, they may never find this place."

"That's the idea/the idea," said two voices in unison.

Hotshoe and Annie and Laura turned to see two sets of cold, menacing eyes.

Collect all the
NASCAR Pole Position Adventures:

#1 ROLLING THUNDER
#2 IN THE GROOVE
#3 RACE READY
#4 SPEED DEMON *
#5 HAMMER DOWN *

* coming soon

RACE READY

POLE POSITION ADVENTURES NO. 3

T. B. Calhoun

HarperEntertainment
A Division of HarperCollinsPublishers

for J. Sam Johnson, who taught me to love cars

▟ HarperEntertainment

A Division of HarperCollins*Publishers*
10 East 53ʳᵈ Street, New York, N.Y. 10022-5299

First printing: December 1998

Cover illustrations by John Youssi © 1998
Designed by Jeannette Jacobs

Printed in the United States of America

ISBN 0–06–105959–5

98 99 00 01 02 10 9 8 7 6 5 4 3 2 1

CONTENTS

DEAD MAN'S CURVE

It was called Dead Man's Curve.

It lay near the bottom of a long hill in the Tennessee mountains.

The highway curved sharply around a rocky cliff overlooking a steep ravine.

Two men waited, hidden in the rocks.

Between them was a plastic garbage can filled with used motor oil.

"I hear somethin' coming!" said Belvis Bewley.

"I hear it, too!" said Broadus Bewley.

"Get the stuff ready," said Belvis.

"It's ready!" said Broadus.

Belvis and Broadus Bewley were brothers. They had lived near Dead Man's Curve for years, on a tiny farm cut into the mountainside.

1

It was hard to make a living farming in the Tennessee mountains. Belvis and Broadus didn't care. They didn't like farming anyway. Neither did their mule, Katy, who was waiting in the trees below the rocks.

They had figured out an easier way of making a living.

Every morning they waited by the road for tourists from out of state. They poured oil on the road, so the tourists' car would slide off into the ravine.

Then Belvis and Broadus would appear, as if by magic, with their mule Katy to pull the car out of the ravine.

For a price!

"It sounds like a truck to me," said Belvis.

"Darn," said Broadus.

Belvis and Broadus didn't like trucks. Truck drivers were tough and independent, and sometimes they saw through the scheme. Once, Belvis had gotten a black eye when he had tried to collect from a trucker they had "helped" out of the ravine.

Belvis peered over the rocks to see what fate was sending his brother and himself that day.

2

He could hear a big engine straining. If it was a car, it was pulling a big load. More likely it was a truck, in which case they would let it go.

Then he saw it at the top of the hill.

"Hot dog," said Belvis. "It's one of them big RV campers!"

"Goody!" said Broadus.

What luck! A big, lumbering, unwieldy RV—recreational vehicle—probably with a retired couple from Michigan or Indiana inside! The woman would have gray hair in a beehive and jeweled glasses. The man would wear blue pants and white shoes, and maybe a captain's hat.

After they went off the road, they would be scared—then nervous—then grateful. They would willingly fork over lots of greenbacks for "assistance."

"Piece of cake!" said Belvis.

"Goody!" said Broadus. He tipped over the barrel so the dirty black flowed down the rocks and across the narrow asphalt road, making it dangerously slick.

Now all Belvis and Broadus Bewley had to do was wait!

● ● ● ● ●

"You know the rule," said Hotshoe.

"Okay, okay," said Laura Travis, clicking her seat belt into place.

The rule was that the Travis kids had to wear seat belts when they rode in the front of their grandfather's RV. In the back, sitting around the table or watching TV, they could do without.

"Tired of watching TV?" asked Hotshoe.

"Tired of listening to boy talk," said Laura. "All Kin and Laptop ever talk about is cars and computers, cars and computers. I thought I'd come up here and keep my grandpa company for a while."

"Good idea," said Hotshoe.

His RV was laboring slowly up a steep road in the Tennessee mountains. Laura and her two brothers, Kin and Laptop, were orphans whose parents had been killed in a tragic plane crash only a year before. Their wealthy Aunt Adrian in Boston, their official guardian, had sent them to spend the summer with their grandfather, Hotshoe Hunter. Hotshoe was retired from racing, but in the old days he had been a crackerjack driver. Now all he drove was his RV—and the classic 1955 Chevy towed behind it. He followed the NASCAR racing circuit, selling custom camshafts and hanging out with his old buddies, all of whom were racers.

He and his grandchildren were on their way from the Pine Gap Raceway in Tennessee to a high school gym in North Carolina, where Laura was going to play her first country music concert.

"Where are all the other NASCAR drivers and their huge vans and car-haulers?" Laura asked. "I thought we all left the race track at about the same time."

"We did," said Hotshoe. "But I took a shortcut. This road leads to Rockcastle Mountain, by way of Dead Man's Curve. Most of the others don't know about it."

"Dead Man's Curve!" Laura gave a little shiver. The deep woods beside the road looked spooky. "Are you sure this is the best way to go?"

"It's just a name!" Hotshoe said as the RV topped the hill. "It doesn't really mean anything."

He shifted gears and picked up speed as the RV started down a long, steep grade.

"Names mean something," said Laura. "Is that the curve at the bottom of the hill? It looks funny to me."

"What the…?!" muttered Hotshoe.

———————————————————

Something was on the road ahead.

It looked like an oil slick, spreading across the pavement.

And he was going almost 70!

"Your move," said Laptop

"Give me time!" said Kin. "Give me time!"

Kin was trying to play chess. Kin was fifteen, but his little brother Larry—or Laptop, as he preferred to be called—was a lot better at games.

That was the weird thing about little kids. Their brains were still elastic, like bubble gum. They caught on too quickly. Kin had made the mistake of teaching Laptop chess, and now Laptop was beating him.

Kin didn't want to think about chess anyway. He preferred thinking about stock car racing, which he had just discovered. The last few days at Pine Gap Raceway had been the most exciting of his life.

He had made a new friend, Junior Peytona. Junior's dad, Waddy Peytona, was a NASCAR driver. Next weekend Kin would be working as a member of Waddy's pit crew in a real race, in North Carolina.

He could hardly wait.

Meanwhile, it was a long drive over the mountains in Grandpa Hotshoe's big RV. And there was nothing to do but play chess. Kin and Laptop were playing at the RV's dinette table while their sister, Laura, rode up front with their granddad.

"Go on and move," said Laptop.

"Okay, okay!" said Kin.

He moved his bishop to what looked like a good spot.

"Check," said Laptop.

"No way!" said Kin.

"Way!" said Laptop. With a grin, he showed his big brother how he had left his king open to attack.

Kin groaned. He was studying the board, trying to figure out how to save his king, when all of a sudden the RV tilted to one side.

The chess pieces fell to the floor.

Laptop flew across the room, and Kin was right behind him.

"Worf!" Their little dog, Scuffs, tumbled ears over tail.

Kin looked out the window.

The world was spinning around and around.

He saw a rocky cliff, then trees, then the cliff again, then trees . . .

The RV was in a spin, sliding toward the edge of the highway, which dropped off into a deep ravine.

IN THE SPIN

"Hang on!" said Hotshoe.

It was definitely an oil slick, and it was spreading all the way across the road.

The black oil covered a sharp turn at the bottom of a long hill. On one side of the highway was a rocky cliff; on the other, a drop-off into a steep ravine.

Hotshoe pumped his brakes, trying to lose all the speed he could before hitting the oil; then he let off the brakes at the last moment.

The huge RV skated across the oil, then began to spin.

Laura watched, horrified, as the trees and rocks swapped places, again and again.

"Hang on, honey!" cried her grandfather as he wrestled with the wheel.

9

He spun the wheel, trying to keep the front end and the back in alignment. But his instincts, honed by years of racing, told him it was too late. The RV was out of control.

Hotshoe knew his only chance was to throw it into gear and try to pull out when he hit the narrow strip of dirt and gravel at the edge of the ravine.

If he gave it enough power he might, just possibly, pull out before the crash.

Maybe . . .

"What a bad sport!" cried Laptop.

"I didn't knock the board over, we're crashing!" cried Kin. "Hang on!"

He had envied race car drivers their speed. Now he envied them their roll bars, crash helmets, and seat belts—all the safety devices NASCAR requires to keep stock car racing safe.

Outside the window, the rocks and trees continued to swap places as the RV spun around and around.

Atop the rocks on the other side of the highway, Kin thought he saw two men and a mule.

Then they were gone and the ravine was rushing closer and closer. . . .

"Oh, dear!" said Laura.

Her first thought was of the Wabash Cannonball guitar in the closet in the back of the RV.

Laura had never played guitar until a few nights before, when Infield Annie, one of Hotshoe's friends, had given her the guitar her mother had played as a little girl. Laura was surprised to find that her fingers knew the chords, and her voice knew the words, to every country song.

It was like magic! The guitar was the key to Laura's music, and she worried more about its safety than her own.

She watched in horror through the windshield as the RV spun across the highway between the cliff and the ravine.

What was that in the rocks?

A mule?

Two men with a barrel . . . ?

"Hang on!" Laptop whispered.

He was talking to his Apricot 07 laptop computer, which he clutched against his chest as the RV swapped ends again and again, sliding inexorably toward the ravine.

Laptop and his computer had been in tight spots before. At the Pine Gap Raceway he had been kidnapped, and he had escaped by parasailing out of a car hanging under a blimp. His computer had fallen two thousand feet and survived (luckily landing in a pot of greens).

But this looked worse.

Much worse.

Laptop hung on to the leg of the dinette table as the world spun around out the window.

He saw trees . . . rocks . . . and what was that—

A mule?

"Worf!"

"Worf is right!" said Kin as he picked up the little dog, who was sliding across the linoleum floor like a skater. A bad skater—colliding first with one wall, and then with the other.

Scuffs and Kin had adopted each other at the race track, where Scuffs had saved the day by finding and fixing a problem with Waddy Peytona's race car.

Scuffs was a smart little dog.

But his instincts were even better than his brain.

And as he cowered in Kin's arms, watching the world spin around outside the window, Scuffs saw something that made his hair stand on end.

Two men were standing on the rocks by the road.

They were grinning.

To a dog, there is nothing more evil than an evil human's grin!

"Worf!" said Scuffs. He had to warn Kin and the rest of the Travis kids about the bad men!

Just then there was a loud *crunch!*

The RV hit the gravel at the side of the road . . . and began to tip dangerously.

"What if they're killed?" Broadus asked Belvis. "That RV is so big, it just might crash through the trees and fall all the way to the bottom of the ravine."

"Even better," said Belvis. "Then we can loot the RV, recover the bodies, and collect a reward for our humanitarian efforts."

━ ━ ━ ━ ━ ━ ━ ━ ━ ━ ━ ━ ━ ━ ━ ━ ━ ━

"I like your thinkin'," said Broadus. "There they go, over the side!"

The RV hung on two wheels, teetering on the edge of the ravine.

With practiced skill from years of driving on dirt tracks, Hotshoe heel-and-toed, hitting the brakes to slide the rear end around, downshifting into second, and revving the engine all in one swift motion.

At the last instant, as the RV hung over the ravine, he popped the clutch.

The huge vehicle straightened and slipped forward, even as it was sliding sideways.

"Hang on!" cried Hotshoe to his grandchildren.

"We're trying!" answered Kin from the back.

"Game over," whispered Laptop, who was sure they were goners.

"Oh, dear," said Laura, still worried about her guitar.

"Worf," said Scuffs.

Gravel crunched . . . tires screamed on asphalt . . . the big engine roared, and at the last possible instant, using the last inch of gravel, the RV righted itself and sped straight down the highway, out of the oil slick.

(14)

• • • • •

"Darn," said Belvis.

"Double darn," said Broadus. "What kind of drivin' was that? I never saw nobody handle a vehicle like that."

"Pretty fancy, all right," said Belvis. He clucked at the mule. "Come on, Katy, we'll try again tomorrow."

As the RV sped out of sight down the road, the two men and the mule headed dejectedly for home.

"Maybe we'll have better luck tomorrow," said Broadus.

"Maybe our luck was better than we know," said Belvis.

"What do you mean?"

"I'm not sure I want to tangle with whoever was driving that RV," said Belvis. "Maybe we're lucky they got away."

"Whew!" said Hotshoe. "That's the closest call I've had since that little dirt track in Indiana twenty years ago."

"Oh, Grandpa Hotshoe!" said Laura. Impulsively she sprang out of her seat and threw her arms around her grandfather. "You saved us!"

"Get back in your seat, honey," Hotshoe replied, embarrassed. "You know the rules."

"Hooray," applauded Kin and Laptop from the back.

"Worf," said Scuffs.

"What caused that slide?" Kin asked.

"An oil slick," said Hotshoe.

"I'll bet bandits put it there!" said Laptop. "I saw some suspicious-looking characters on top of those rocks."

"Me too," said Kin.

"Me too!" said Laura.

"Nonsense!" said Hotshoe. "You kids have been watching too much television."

"How did that oil get there, then?" asked Laura.

"Somebody probably sprung a leak, that's all," said Hotshoe. "You kids have lived in the city too long. You're too suspicious. Most country people are as honest as the day is long. Nobody would deliberately cause a wreck just to make a little money."

"Speaking of the city," said Laura. "I just thought of something. We forgot to return Aunt Adrian's call! She left a message saying to call her back ASAP."

"Let's forget it," said Kin. "She probably wants us to come back to Boston. Do you want to go back?"

"Not particularly," said Laura. "I'm getting to like the South."

"Me three," said Laptop from the back of the RV.

"Worf," said Scuffs.

"Maybe you should let sleeping dogs lie," said Hotshoe.

"What does that mean?" asked Laura.

"It means just pretend we never got the message."

"That's a little irresponsible," said Laura.

But the idea was tempting. Aunt Adrian's elegant house was so cold and quiet. And the NASCAR racing circuit was so warm and full of life!

"Checkmate," said Laptop.

"What?!?"

Kin turned around, and to his surprise, saw the chess board set up with all the pieces back in place.

"Who did that?" he asked.

"Worf," said Scuffs.

"No way," said Kin.

"Just play," said Laptop.

"Okay, okay!" said Kin, handing his little brother his king. "You win again."

"Hey!" said Laura from the front of the RV. "I think I know that song!"

WILD KINGDOM

"Beautiful," said Laura.

"Awesome," said Laptop.

"Not bad," said Kin.

They were standing with their grandfather in a scenic view area, overlooking a deep green valley filled with trees.

Above them was the craggy ridge of Rockcastle Mountain. It was the same mountain Laptop had seen from above when he had been abducted in a blimp from the Pine Gap Raceway. Later, he had flown over the mountain in a helicopter with Wild Bill Wilde and State Trooper Thom, looking for Wild Bill's stolen Studebaker car, but without success.

The mountain had looked wild and beautiful from above. From below, it looked even better.

Best of all was a waterfall that flowed from a cave under the cliffs that ringed the mountaintop.

"It's called Sudden Falls," said Hotshoe. "It drops a thousand feet down the mountain, then flows right through the little town of Sudden Falls, North Carolina. In fact, it flows right near the high school gymnasium where Laura will be performing tonight.

"Not Laura," said Laura.

"Huh?" asked all three guys at once.

"I need a stage name," Laura said. "Something better than just Laura. Something dramatic. Something suitable for going on stage and performing for thousands of eager fans."

"Why don't you just call yourself Miss Bighead," Kin suggested helpfully.

"Yeah," said Laptop.

"I was only kidding," protested Laura.

"Knock it off, kids," said Hotshoe.

"Hey, here they come!" said Kin.

He pointed toward the highway. Several enormous car-haulers painted with racing colors and sponsors' trademarks were pulling into the scenic view area.

"About time!" said Hotshoe.

Several cars and motorcycles that had been traveling with the haulers pulled in behind them. Steve Gregson was riding a 1200cc Harley. A Mustang pulled up beside him, and Kin was thrilled to be introduced to NASCAR legend Bill Elliott, "Awesome Bill from Dawsonville."

"What took you boys so long?" Hotshoe taunted.

"Oh, knock it off, Hotshoe," joked Elliott. "You're the only one racing. We're all just cruising, taking a day off."

"Hotshoe probably found a shortcut anyway," joked Gregson. "He's always cutting across the infield."

"If you only knew!" said Laura—and she told them the story of the oil-slick road.

"That must have been the Bewley brothers," said Elliott, shaking his head. "Two guys with a mule?"

"Yes," said Kin.

"Some day the law will catch up to those two," said Bill Elliott. "If an angry truck driver doesn't get them first. There's nothing worse than criminals who prey on honest folks!"

"I agree," said Laptop.

"Worf," said Scuffs.

"I thought you said country people were honest!" said Kin. He looked at his grandfather and shook his head.

"I didn't say *all*," Hotshoe protested. "I said *most*."

Hotshoe was scanning the valley with his binoculars.

"There's a hawk," he said to Kin, handing him the binoculars.

"He's diving!" said Kin. "Bingo! He got a mouse."

Kin handed the binoculars to Laura, who was standing with Laptop by the low wall overlooking the valley.

Laura took one look through the powerful binoculars and shivered. "Ugh!"

She sympathized with the mouse.

"Let me have a look," said Laptop.

He put the binoculars to his eyes and saw the mouse struggling to get out of the hawk's claws.

The struggle reminded him of his adventure when he had been in the classic car kidnapped by a blimp. He had managed to get away and paraglide to safety.

The mouse was struggling harder and harder. Finally it slipped loose.

"Way to go!" yelled Laptop.

He watched as the mouse fell free. The hawk looked down, disappointed.

The mouse dropped further and further.

And Laptop realized that the mouse's story wasn't going to have a happy ending like his own.

The mouse didn't have a parachute!

He looked away at the last moment, then handed the binoculars to his grandfather.

"Neat stuff, huh?" said Hotshoe.

"Not really," said Laptop. "I think nature is gross."

I agree, thought Laura silently.

More and more NASCAR car-haulers pulled in. Others labored on toward the high pass that would take them over the top of the mountain, into North Carolina.

The big car-haulers were beautiful, and Kin felt thrilled to be part of the racing world.

"So I hear you're working with Waddy's crew," said Bill Elliott.

"I'm going to be working in the pit," Kin said. "But I want to be a driver, like you."

Elliott is one of NASCAR's all-time greats, with forty career wins.

"I think if you want to be a driver, the best place to start is in the shop, where you learn the basics of how a car is put together." said Elliott. "Then you need to spend some time in the pits, where you can see how the mechanics are applied under actual race conditions. Remember, Kin, the driver doesn't just point the car around the track. He listens, feels, and thinks. Then he reports back to the other members of his crew on what is wrong and what is right. If you want to be a NASCAR driver, you have to know suspensions, tires, engines, transmissions . . . "

Kin groaned. "By the time I learn all that, I'll be too old to drive!"

"You better not let Waddy hear you say that," said Elliott. He grinned and pointed to the highway.

"Speak of the devil!"

Waddy Peytona's trailer pulled in and gave a big blast on the air horn. The head mechanic, Tach, was driving. He waved.

A Cadillac pulled in behind the trailer. Waddy and Junior got out with Cope, the crew chief.

Someone else was with them. A stranger.

Someone Kin had never met.

A girl!

"Teresa, this is my friend Kin," said Junior.

"Glad to meet you," Teresa said, sticking out one perfect little hand.

"Uh—uh—uh, hello," said Kin, retreating backward. While he shook hands awkwardly, he squinted at the girl. It was like looking into the sun.

He turned to Junior. "You didn't tell me you had a girlfriend."

"Girlfriend?" Junior laughed. "Teresa's my kid sister!"

Kid sister? Kin thought. *You call that a kid sister?* He looked across the lot at Laura, who he loved and everything, but, well . . .

That was a kid sister.

This, this beautiful, violet-eyed tomboy in a Waddy Peytona Racing Team uniform; this laughing girl with honey blond hair tied back in a ponytail . . .

This was something else!

"Don't let him fool you, Kin," said Teresa. "Junior calls me his kid sister because I was born three minutes after he was."

Kin looked at her and comprehension began to dawn.

"We're twins!" said Junior with a laugh.

Soon it was time to go.

"Worf," said Scuffs when he saw Kin getting into the Cadillac with Waddy and his family.

"Don't worry," said Kin to the anxious little dog. "I'm just going to ride with Junior and Teresa over the mountain. To save weight."

"Save weight—I'm sure!" said Laura and Laptop together. They had seen Kin staring at Teresa.

Kin ignored them and petted Scuffs. "You go on and ride in the RV with Grandpa Hotshoe and Laptop and Laura."

"Worf."

"Laura, honey, why don't you ride with me," said Infield Annie, who had just pulled in. "Keep an old lady company."

Annie's VW bus was the slowest vehicle in the caravan.

"Maybe . . ." said Laura. Always responsible, she looked toward her grandfather, who was starting up his RV.

"You go on, honey," he said. "Keep Annie company. Laptop will ride with me."

"Worf!"

"And Scuffs, of course. Come on, boys. We have a long haul to make before evening."

He pointed up at the bulk of Rockcastle Mountain.

"We have to cross over the shoulder of the mountain. We'll be at over thirty-five hundred feet at the crest there. Those car-haulers will have a fairly easy time of it if they gear down, but we'll be slower.

"How come?" asked Laptop.

"They are diesels, built for long hauls," said Hotshoe. "Plus, this RV of mine is pulling extra weight."

He pointed at the 1955 Chevy attached to the back by a tow bar.

"Don't you always tow it?" asked Laptop.

"No way," said Hotshoe. "I usually leave it here in Tennessee, with a friend who has a little farm outside Greeneville. But with all this classic car theft going on, I'm afraid to let my little Chevy out of my sight."

"It's out of your sight when you are towing it,"

---

said Laptop. "The rearview mirrors don't show the area right behind the RV."

"You take things too literally," said Hotshoe. "I may not have it in sight when I'm towing it, but I know exactly where it is."

Or so he thought!

SHIFTING DOWN

There is a range of mountains that covers the entire eastern half of the United States, from New England all the way down to northern Alabama and Georgia.

They are called the Appalachians, and they are among the oldest mountains in the world.

Unlike people, mountains get smaller as they get older. The Appalachians are only about half as high as the younger Rockies, out West. They are a lot less rugged, too. They have been worn away by millions of years of wind and rain.

Not as high.

Not as steep.

But still plenty awesome, thought Laptop as Hotshoe's massive GM-powered RV labored up the long hill toward the high shoulder of Rockcastle Mountain.

"What does the tach read?" asked Hotshoe. He thought he would take this opportunity to teach Laptop a thing or two about driving and engines.

Laptop scanned the dashboard until he found the dial marked TACHOMETER.

"It reads 3400," he said. "Thirty-four hundred what? Inches per hour? Does it tell us how fast we are going?"

"Nope," said Hotshoe. "It tells us how fast the engine is going. The 3400 is rpm's, or revolutions per minute. That's how fast the engine is turning over."

"Three thousand times a minute!" said Laptop. "That's awesome."

"Not really," said Hotshoe. "In a race, the engines turn over between seven and eight thousand rpm's."

"Now we've dropped to 2800," said Laptop. "How fast does that mean we are going?"

"Depends on what gear we're in," said Hotshoe. "Check the speedometer. What does it say right now?"

Laptop leaned over to look. "Forty-three— that's miles per hour, right?"

"Right, unless it's in kilometers, which are a little more than half a mile."

"It's dropping," said Laptop. "Now it's just 41."

"Watch what happens when I shift down," said Hotshoe.

He clutched and raced the engine as he threw the gearshift lever into third.

The truck was still going 41, but now the engine was racing at 3700 rpm.

"I see!" said Laptop. "You shifted down, into a lower gear. That means the engine runs faster for the same speed."

"Exactly," said Hotshoe. "And that gives it more power for the long pull. An engine doesn't want to run too slow. That's called lugging. Too fast is called over-revving. Both are hard on an engine, but lugging is worse. Every engine has a range where it likes to run. For a race car that might be between 6000 and 8000. For this old GM eight, it's between 2500 and 4000."

"Rpm's are dropping again," said Laptop, watching the tachometer closely.

"That's probably because the road is getting steeper," said Hotshoe. "Let me know when they drop below 2200. Then I'll shift down again."

"Aye, aye, sir," said Laptop, one eye on the tach and the other on the road.

"What a great view!" said Kin.

They were at the top of Rockcastle Mountain. The road now led down a long valley into North Carolina. At the bottom, he could see the roofs and streets of a tiny town.

"That's Sudden Falls down there," said Waddy. "That's where your little sister's going to play tonight."

"I can't wait," said Teresa.

"Really?" asked Kin.

"I love country music," said Teresa. "Don't you?"

"Uh—sure," said Kin. He was having a hard time thinking. Every time he looked into Teresa's violet eyes he felt confused, muddled, empty-headed.

What was happening to him?

He was afraid he knew.

Two motorcycles roared by, heading down the hill toward Tennessee. They were powerful trail bikes. A man rode on one and a woman on the other. They wore silver jumpsuits emblazoned with scarlet lightning bolts.

"Japanese iron," said Waddy's crew chief. "Copacetic!"

"I thought you liked nothing but Harleys, Cope," said Waddy.

"I'm a patriotic American," said Cope. "But that doesn't mean I can't admire foreign iron."

"Especially when it's *copacetic*," said Kin, laughing.

The big rig passed a small side road.

"There's the turnoff for the falls," said Teresa. "I wish we could stop and have a look."

"We'll see it from the bottom," said Waddy. "I want to get on down to the town, so we can get a good night's rest and make it on into Charlotte tomorrow."

"Aye, aye, Captain," said Junior, who was driving. He started the long descent.

"Quite a parade," said Infield Annie as she watched the first of the big rigs go over the top of the mountain.

In the lead was Bill Elliott's giant car-hauler. Just behind them was Waddy's aging team transporter. Wabash Guitars had promised him a new one, once the season was over. But that was several races away. In the meantime, the Ford-powered rig labored up the mountain with "a lot of heart and a little compression," as Waddy liked to say.

At the end of the long line of colorful NASCAR rigs came Hotshoe Hunter's lumbering RV, with MERLIN MIXMASTER CAMSHAFT WIZARDRY painted on the side. Hotshoe was near the back because he knew his rig was slow.

Infield Annie, who was the slowest of all, went last.

Let the boys race, Annie thought to herself. *I'm glad I'm last. I wouldn't want all those huge rigs rushing to get by me.*

The traffic coming down the mountain was light. A pickup or two, a car filled with tourists enjoying the beautiful mountain scenery.

And two motorcyclists—

They rode powerful trail bikes with knobby tires. They wore sleek silver suits with lightning bolts on them.

Laura watched enviously as they coasted down the long hill, the spokes of their wheels flashing in the sun.

"That looks like fun," she said to Annie.

"A motorcycle's like a bad marriage," said Annie. "It's fast and fun, until you hit bad weather. Then you realize how unprotected you are."

Is this the voice of experience? Laura wondered.

"Eighteen hundred rpm's," said Laptop. "Better shift down again."

Hotshoe shifted down to second. The engine labored strongly, pulling like a faithful mule in wet clay. It wouldn't go fast, but it wouldn't stop either, even if he had to shift all the way down to first gear.

Behind, he could see Infield Annie's Volkswagen mobile kitchen, filled with pots and pans and folding chairs.

Plus one girl—Hotshoe could see his granddaughter Laura sitting in front, the sun gleaming off her cornstalk yellow hair.

"What a pretty girl," thought Hotshoe. "She looks so much like her mother."

Hotshoe had lost a lot, but he had a lot to be thankful for: his grandchildren, whom he was finally getting to know. His racing memories, his NASCAR friends, his Merlin camshaft business.

And best of all, his classic 1955 Chevy! Since it was directly behind the trailer, it was out of sight of his rearview mirrors. But he knew it was there, safe and sound.

Yes, he had a lot be thankful for. While he was musing on all this, two motorcycles sped past, heading down the mountain.

"They look familiar," said Laptop.

"Dirt bikes," said Hotshoe. "They'll go anywhere."

"I don't mean the bikes," said Laptop. "I mean the riders." Then he noticed the tach. "Your rpm's are dropping again, Grandpa. They're down to 2100. Can you shift gears again?"

"I'd rather not," said Hotshoe. "That would put me all the way down into low gear. Let's see if she'll hold at this speed. The hill doesn't look too much steeper ahead."

"Didn't they just pass us going the other way?" Annie asked.

Two motorcycles were roaring around Annie's VW bus, heading up the long hill.

"That's definitely the same two that came down the hill a moment ago," said Annie.

"Maybe they missed their turn or something," Laura said.

The two bikes cut in between Annie's straining VW and Hotshoe's laboring RV. The sign on the back of the RV read: IF YOU CAN'T SEE MY MIRRORS, I CAN'T SEE YOU!

The two motorcyclists then pulled up alongside the towed Chevy, one on each side, where they were out of sight of Hotshoe's rearview mirrors.

With a quick *blat! blat!* of their powerful engines, they caught up to the rear bumper of the RV, where the tow bar was attached.

"What the—" Annie said.

"What the . . . !!" echoed Laura.

They stared in amazement as the riders leaned over and unhooked the tow bar from the back of the RV.

"Look out!" said Annie.

The Chevy rolled free, cut loose from the RV.

But it wasn't about to crash. Moving in perfect unison, like circus performers, the two motorcyclists grabbed the tow bar. One on each side, they steered the Chevy off the highway—into the thick brush.

Laura blinked—and they were gone! "We're witnessing a crime in broad daylight!" she cried.

"Hotshoe! Laptop!" Annie was shouting. She banged on the dashboard of her VW in frustration.

But of course it did no good; there was no way Hotshoe and Laptop could hear her.

"The horn," said Laura. "Try the horn."

"That's better!" said Laptop. "The rpm's are picking up again. Twenty-two hundred. Twenty-three hundred."

"Hmmmm," said Hotshoe. "I felt a little surge of power just then, like the secondary barrels on the carburetor just kicked in."

"I felt the surge, too," said Laptop.

"One problem," said Hotshoe. "There are no secondaries on this carburetor."

"Well, whatever it is, we're going better than ever. You're actually picking up speed in second gear."

"Maybe the road leveled out a little," Hotshoe speculated. "It's sure odd for an engine to have a surge of power like that. It's almost like we picked up an extra fifty horsepower, or lost a few thousand pounds of weight. What's that noise?"

"Somebody's honking," said Laptop.

Hotshoe looked out the window, into his rearview mirror.

"It's Annie. She's waving at me to pull over. She must be having engine trouble."

WELCOME TO SUDDEN FALLS

The little town of Sudden Falls, North Carolina, was nestled in a hollow at the foot of Rockcastle Mountain.

It was no more than a single wide street lined with four motels, two on each side, a souvenir shop, a high school, a video rental store, and a McDonald's.

"Copacetic," said Cope as the Cadillac rolled in off the highway. "No town is complete without a video rental store."

As soon as they were parked, Cope ran across the street into the video store.

"Guess he doesn't like country music," said Kin as he and Junior and Teresa piled out of the car. "If he rents a video, he'll miss my sister's show tonight."

"Cope'll be there," said Junior. "He never rents videos."

"He's too cheap," said Teresa. "He just reads the boxes and looks at the pictures."

Kin was glad to be out in the open air; it had been a long ride over the mountain. He stretched and looked around.

On one side the little town nestled against the steep slope of Rockcastle Mountain. On the other three sides were rolling hills covered with thick forests of hardwood and pine.

"All the trees of the East are here," said Junior, who spent most of his spare time reading about nature and geography.

"All?" asked his twin sister Teresa, the eternal skeptic.

"Almost all, anyway," said Junior. "In the mountains, every thousand feet you go up is like going seven hundred miles north. So the mountains include just about every ecology from Canada to North Carolina."

"No palm trees, though," said Teresa.

"Who needs palm trees?" said Junior.

"Me," said Teresa. "I'm a creature of the sun." She raised her sunglasses to show her laughing eyes.

Kin pretended to yawn and look around at the scenery. He couldn't stop looking at Teresa, but he didn't want her to know it. Was it her violet eyes? Her ponytail?

It didn't matter. Kin knew what it was, and he knew what to do about it. He knew what he was feeling, and he intended to stop it before it got started.

Love! In the movies and on TV it only led to trouble. Love made guys act like total idiots.

It had to be avoided at all costs.

It was important to look bored. Kin pretended to yawn again.

"What are you doing, trying to catch flies?" Teresa asked with a laugh. "Come on, let's look around the town."

"Where's this music barn where your sister is going to play?" asked Junior as he and Kin and Teresa walked along the town's short Main Street.

"Beats me," said Kin.

"It's the high school gym," said a familiar voice. "We've rented it for the big event."

They turned and saw Hollis Wabash III, the guitar mogul, getting out of his pink Cadillac.

"Where is your sister?" he asked Kin. "We need

to get started on sound checks and setup for the show tonight."

"Oh, she'll be along," said Kin. "She's riding with Infield Annie and Grandpa Hotshoe. They were at the end of our little caravan."

"They were slooooow!" said Teresa. "They're probably just now at the top of the mountain."

"Unless they hurry, they'll have a hard time finding a parking place," said Waddy Peytona, joining them. He, too, was stretching after the long ride over the mountain. "Look at these monsters rolling in."

Hollis Wabash III stopped to shake hands with a man who was crossing the street. Hollis introduced him as the mayor of Sudden Falls.

"Hope we're not cluttering up your town, Mayor," said Waddy, always polite. He looked around at the huge car-haulers that were still arriving off the highway. The tiny town looked as if it were being invaded by dinosaurs.

The mayor smiled genially. "Not at all," he said. "We are honored to be a stop on the NASCAR circuit, even if it's not for racing."

"This musical program to honor NASCAR families may end up being part of the regular tour," said Hollis Wabash III. "And look—here's our warmup act. I think."

He looked dubious. A 1950 Ford "woody" drove up and parked in front of the Sudden Falls High School gym. Four gnarly-looking dudes piled out.

"Surf's up!" one said.

"Huh?" asked Hollis Wabash III and Waddy and the mayor.

"Huh?" echoed Kin and Junior and Teresa.

"We're the Beach Dudes," said the tallest of the four. He wore denim cutoffs and a SHARKS ARE PEO-PLE TOO T-shirt. "We're your warmup band."

"Our what?" asked a startled Hollis Wabash III.

"Your warmup band. For the gig tonight."

"There's been some mistake," said Hollis Wabash III. "I hired an all-girl a cappella country vocal group called Peach Stew."

MOTORCYCLE PIRATES

"It's impossible," said Hotshoe. "It's just impossible."

It seemed to make him feel better to say it, so no one argued with him.

Even though it was not only possible, but certain.

Someone had certainly stolen the '55 Chevrolet.

It was gone.

Hotshoe and Laptop were standing on the side of the highway, behind the parked RV. Annie's VW bus was pulled in behind the RV, and Annie and Laura were standing beside Hotshoe.

All of them had shocked, long faces.

Gone!

"So it was the two on the motorcycles," said Laptop. "I thought they looked familiar. They were the same air pirates who stole Wild Bill's Studebaker!"

"Motorcycle pirates now," muttered Infield Annie. She patted Hotshoe on the shoulder. She hated to see her old friend suffer.

"That makes me so mad!" said Laura. "We watched them unhook it and then pull off the road. They went off into these funny little bushes."

She pointed to the tracks of the car and the motorcycles, which led off the highway under a canopy of low, brushy trees.

"Those 'funny little bushes,' as you call them, are rhododendron," said Annie. "Mountain laurel, we call it. It grows wild all through these hills."

"Let's concentrate on finding my Chevy," said Hotshoe. "Save the botany lesson for later."

"Let's go, then," said Laura. "They left a trail for us to follow!"

She started into the laurel thicket, following the tire tracks.

"Wait!"

She turned and looked at her grandfather.

"We aren't going in there until we take some precautions," said Hotshoe. "We don't know if they are armed, or what."

"They're armed all right!" said Laptop. "At least

they were when they were climbing down the rope from the blimp after me!"

"In that case . . . you all wait here."

Hotshoe ducked into his RV. When he emerged seconds later, he was carrying a huge, old-fashioned pistol.

"Looks like a pirate gun," said Laptop. "Perfect for pirates."

"Is that a real gun?" Laura asked.

"I thought you didn't carry a gun," said Annie, sounding disgusted. Like many people all over the world, she didn't think guns were particularly cool or neat or beautiful.

"You know I don't," said Hotshoe. "I keep this one in a box. It's a nineteenth-century Scottish black powder pistol. Cap and ball. A souvenir."

"Is it loaded?" asked Laptop.

"It soon will be."

While the kids and Annie watched, Hotshoe poured black powder from a plastic bottle into the barrel of the ancient gun. Then he wrapped a lead ball in a patch of greasy paper and jammed it down the barrel with a short metal rod.

"Cap and ball?" asked Laura. "You mean there's no bullet?"

"The lead ball is the bullet," said Hotshoe. "The powder goes in first, then the ball, with the wadding to keep it tight in the barrel." He pulled back the hammer and put a little brass cap under it. "This little brass cap, called a percussion cap, is what sets off the powder."

"Like a cap in a cap gun?" asked Laptop.

"Exactly," said Hotshoe. "It only has enough power to set off the gunpowder in the barrel. Then—boom!"

"Only one shot?" asked Laptop.

"That's why every shot has to count," said Hotshoe.

"Who are you planning to shoot?" asked Laura.

"Nobody, unless I have to," said Hotshoe, sticking the pistol into his belt. "I never shot anybody, and I don't want to. But these people are dangerous. Laptop can tell you. We've seen them operate. We need to be prepared."

"Why don't we just call the police?" Annie suggested.

"I already did," said Hotshoe, sticking the pistol into his belt. "I called from the cell phone in the trailer, and left a message for Trooper Thom at state police headquarters."

"He's a Tennessee trooper," said Laptop. "Aren't we in North Carolina?"

"The top of the mountain is the state line," said Hotshoe. "I figured it was close enough, and I don't have any North Carolina numbers. But I can't wait for the police, anyway. The trail will get cold."

"Worf!" said Scuffs.

Laptop tucked his computer under his arm and pulled his cap down tight. "Let's get going, then," he said.

"Whoa," said Hotshoe, grabbing Laptop's arm and pulling him back. "There's no *we* about it. You kids wait here with Annie, while I follow these tracks."

"But—" Laura and Laptop said together.

"No *buts* about it," said Hotshoe. He pointed at Scuffs. "The dog stays, too!"

He turned and was gone, into the laurel thicket that ringed the steep crest of Rockcastle Mountain.

STUPID FEELINGS

"What's that?" asked Kin.

Tach and Junior were unloading a four-wheeled motorcycle with fat rear tires from the back of the Waddy Peytona Racing Team carhauler.

"That's an ATV," said Junior. "ATV stands for all terrain vehicle. It's a little go-anywhere machine with a 350cc engine and a four-speed transmission."

"Cc's are cubic centimeters," said Tach. The big, burly African-American mechanic loved explaining engines almost as much as he loved working on them. "Cubic centimeters, liters, and cubic inches are all ways of measuring an engine's *displacement*, which is the volume of air pulled in by the pistons, mixed with fuel, compressed and burned for power."

"It's like Godzilla," said Teresa, who was standing close to Kin—uncomfortably and delightfully close. "Size matters."

"The displacement of an engine is basically the size of the cylinders, added up," Tach said. "A liter's about the size of a quart of milk. Multiply that by five and you get the standard NASCAR engine on our circuit. Cut it in half, and you get about the size of the engine in the ATV."

"Like it?" asked Teresa as she helped steer the gleaming little machine down the ramp. "Want to go for a ride?"

"Hey, great idea!" said Junior. "You've been wanting to start driving, and an ATV is a great way to learn. You are off the road where you can learn handling, and the worst that can happen is you get stuck in the mud."

"Or hit a tree, or fall off a cliff, or . . ." added Tach.

"Okay, okay," said Junior. "We get the idea. It's important to use caution when riding anything, on or off the road. But still, an ATV is great for learning to drive."

The bright blue and yellow ATV had a long banana seat like a motorcycle. Kin got on and put his hands on the handlebars. He could hardly wait to try it.

"Not here," said Waddy, joining them. "You kids take him out in the woods, where he can't hurt anything but a tree."

Kin got off.

Teresa got on.

"I—I thought you were going to take me," Kin said to Junior.

"Teresa's almost as good a driver as I am," said Junior.

"Almost—in your dreams," said Teresa. She grinned back at Kin. "Got a problem with learning from a girl?"

"Uh—no," said Kin. How could he tell her that the problem wasn't that she was a girl, it was that—

It was that she was a girl!

Kin gritted his teeth. He was determined not to fall in love and get stupid. All it took was willpower.

"Of course not," he said. "Girls and boys are the same to me."

"Oh, really," said Junior.

"Shut up, stupid," said Teresa. She patted the seat behind her and Kin got on.

"Teresa, be sure and wear your goggles," Waddy said. "If you lose your contacts, you're blind as a bat."

"Aye, aye, sir!" said Teresa. She hit the starter and the little four-stroke single sprang to life.

Putuputuputuputuputuputuputuput!

She kicked it into gear.

"Where do I hold on?" Kin asked.

"Hold on to me," said Teresa, and she popped the clutch so that the ATV scooted off toward the woods, with its front wheels in the air.

Kin almost fell off the back. He grabbed Teresa's waist just in time.

I'll get over this stupid feeling! he vowed to himself, gritting his teeth. *All it takes is willpower!*

YOU'RE A NATURAL!

"Where is he?" asked Annie, peering into the brush from the highway. "I'm getting worried."

"Me too," said Laura.

"Worf," said Scuffs.

"Let's follow him," said Laptop.

"But he'll get mad," said Laura.

"Let him!" said Annie. It had been almost five minutes since Hotshoe had left. "That hardheaded old fool has to learn that he can't do everything his own way all the time."

The dog went first and Annie followed, with Laptop and Laura right behind. The tire tracks in the soft mud wound through the laurel thicket, around the side of the mountain.

The three were surprised to catch up with

Hotshoe after only a few hundred yards.

He was sitting on a log, with his chin in his hands, looking puzzled and angry. He didn't seem angry, or even surprised, to see Annie, Laura, and Laptop.

Plus Scuffs.

"The trail just ends!" Hotshoe said. "I can't figure it. Where did those thieves take my car?"

"Brrrr," said Laura. "It's cold here."

"It is cool," said Annie. "Where's that breeze coming from?"

The tracks of the car and motorcycles led past the log where Hotshoe was sitting, out of the laurel thicket, straight to a huge boulder at the bottom of a steep cliff—

And stopped.

"It looks like they drove right through the rock and kept going," said Hotshoe. "But that's impossible, of course."

"Worf," said Scuffs, who, as a dog, didn't know the meaning of the word *impossible*.

He ran to the bottom of the cliff and bit the boulder.

It wobbled.

"What the—?" Hotshoe stood up.

"What the . . . ?!?" Annie, Laura, and Laptop crowded around.

"Worf, worf!" said Scuffs as he yanked at the huge rock with his teeth.

It pulled away and tumbled to one side.

Laptop jumped back, too late, as the massive boulder rolled over his toe.

But it didn't hurt. It was papier-mâché!

Behind the "boulder" was a dark hole the size of a garage door. The tracks led straight in.

"A cave!" said Annie.

"A tunnel," said Hotshoe.

"Awesome," said Laptop.

"Brrrr!" said Laura.

The cool air from the cave made them all shiver.

Hotshoe put his hand on Laptop's shoulder. "Go back to the RV," he said.

"That's not fair!" complained Laptop. "You wouldn't even have found the cave if it hadn't been for us."

"I know," said Hotshoe. "We're all going in together. I just want you to go back to the RV and get a flashlight. And hurry!"

● ● ● ● ●

"Aren't you supposed to be wearing goggles?" Kin asked.

Teresa was expertly guiding the ATV up a rough dirt road, toward the foot of Rockcastle Mountain.

"Yeah, but those old goggles are all scratched," she said. "I can see better without them."

"Whatever," said Kin. "I didn't know you wore contacts, anyway."

"Really?" Teresa turned and looked at him over her shoulder. "Did you think I really had *violet* eyes?"

Yes! Kin thought to himself. *But now that I know you're a phony, there's no danger of falling in love!*

Hotshoe shined his flashlight into the tunnel entrance.

The cave was so dark that it seemed to eat light.

The tire tracks in the soft, sandy floor went straight in, then disappeared around a curve.

"Well, here goes," Hotshoe said.

He stepped in, with his gun in one hand and the flashlight in the other.

Laptop and Laura, side by side, were right behind him.

Annie and Scuffs brought up the rear.

It was cold.

It was dark.

It was scary.

"The first few steps into a cave are always the hardest," said Hotshoe cheerily as he led the little party deeper and deeper into the bowels of Rockcastle Mountain.

"That's not true," Laura whispered to Laptop, who was walking beside her. "It gets harder and harder the farther you go."

The first turn led to another, and then another. Laura hated the feeling of being closed in. She could almost feel the enormous bulk of the mountain all around her. *I would give anything to see the sky right now*, she thought.

They came to a small cavern with stone formations hanging from the ceiling like icicles. "These are *stalactites*, formed by dripping water," said Hotshoe, shining his flashlight across them.

Others on the floor pointed up toward the ceiling. "These on the bottom are *stalagmites*," said Hotshoe.

"I never can keep them straight," said Laura.

"That's because it doesn't matter," said Annie.

"Turn the light off so we can see how dark it is!" said Laptop. Unlike his sister, he was thrilled by the idea of being far underground.

Hotshoe switched off the flashlight.

Total blackness pressed in on every side.

There was no sound except dripping water. And a faint roaring noise in the distance that might have been the highway, or the waterfall.

"Awesome," said Laptop.

"Turn it back on," said Laura, straining to keep her voice calm.

"This must be what it's like to be dead and buried," said Annie.

Hotshoe turned on the flashlight. "Let's go. I think I hear something up ahead."

Teresa pulled the ATV over to the side of the trail and got off.

"The controls are like a motorcycle," she said to Kin. "Backwards from a car. You shift with your foot and clutch and brake with your hand. The throttle is the right handgrip. Twist it away from you for more power."

She showed Kin how to work the clutch lever on the left and the brake lever on the right.

The left foot pedal was the gearshift.

"Up for the higher gears, down for the lower," Teresa said. "Ready to try?"

"You bet," said Kin. He slid forward on the seat and Teresa got on behind. He tried to ignore her arms around his waist.

He let out the clutch and twisted the throttle.

The engine died.

He tried it again.

The engine died again.

"Third time's the charm," said Teresa. "Let the clutch out slowly."

This time it worked. Soon the ATV was moving slowly up the trail. Kin had forgotten all about his being-in-love problem. Driving was much more fun.

"Now shift up to second," said Teresa.

Kin pulled in the clutch, kicked the gearshift up one notch, and released the clutch smoothly, giving the machine gas at the same time.

It jerked a little and sped up.

"You're a natural!" said Teresa. "Now let's head up that trail, toward the falls."

THE PIRATES' LAIR

The tunnel led deeper and deeper into the mountain.

The little party moved slowly, following the flickering cone of Hotshoe's flashlight.

"Can you hear it?" asked Hotshoe.

He stopped, and Laura, Laptop, Annie, and Scuffs all huddled around him.

"Hear what?" Annie asked.

"Listen," said Hotshoe.

In the distance, a faint roaring sound could be heard.

"Sounds like applause," said Laura.

"Sounds like a bad modem connection," said Laptop.

"Sounds like fish frying," said Annie.

"Sounds like race cars to me," said Hotshoe.

"Worf!" said Scuffs.

Laptop checked his Apricot 07 laptop computer. All his satellite connections were useless here. They couldn't penetrate the thick rock surrounding him on all sides.

Hotshoe led the way, with one eye watching the group behind him, and the other alert for danger up ahead.

He kept the flashlight trained on the ceiling, scattering the light to keep the shadows down.

Then suddenly the light was gone.

Or rather, the ceiling was gone.

Hotshoe stopped.

"Where are we?" asked Annie.

Wherearewewherearewewherearewe . . . ?

"Worf," said Scuffs.

Worfworfworf . . .

"Awesome," said Laptop.

Awesomesomesomesome, returned his echo.

And it was awesome, indeed.

They had emerged from the tunnel into a huge underground chamber.

Laptop and Laura watched, amazed, as Hotshoe shone the light around.

The cavern was as big as a gymnasium.

Stalactites hung down from the ceiling, and stalagmites stuck up from the floor. In places they almost met.

A swift, shallow stream flowed through the center of the cavern, and disappeared into a dark hole.

Most amazing of all was what was parked in the center of the cavern, on either side of the stream:

Cars.

Classic cars.

Five of them.

"Looks like a used car lot," said Hotshoe. Even the echoes of his voice had a note of happiness.

For one of them was his 1955 Chevy, unharmed.

There was Wild Bill's Studebaker, too. And three other classics: a 1970 Plymouth Barracuda, a 1957 Ford Fairlane, and a 1968 Corvette.

Five stolen classic cars in all.

"So the blimp *didn't* crash into the mountain," said Hotshoe. "Wild Bill's sweetheart survived."

"I'm glad I was wrong," said Laptop. "But I was sure I saw it heading straight for the cliff. There must be another entrance on the other side of the mountain."

"So this is it," Laura said. "The pirates' secret lair. But where are the pirates?"

"We don't want to know," said Hotshoe. "Let's just hope for now that they're not around."

"Amen," said Annie. "They must have brought the Chevy here and left."

"But we didn't pass them coming in," said Laura. "And I don't see their motorcycles anywhere."

"They may be hidden," said Hotshoe. "We need more light. There's another flashlight in the glove compartment of the Chevy. There may be flashlights in the other cars as well."

"I've got a better idea!" said Laptop.

Soon the cavern was illuminated with the headlights of five cars, all facing in different directions.

"Don't turn them all on," said Hotshoe. "We'll need one of these cars to jump-start the others, in case the lights run down the batteries."

"Aye, aye, sir," said Laptop. He ran back over to Hotshoe's Chevy and turned off the headlights.

From the car, he saw that Annie, Laura, and Hotshoe were standing by the stream, which was narrow enough to jump. They were peering down into the hole where the water disappeared.

"Worf," said Scuffs. With his nose to the ground, he ran across the cavern. A second tunnel led off into the darkness.

Laptop saw tire tracks leading out of the tunnel.

"That must be the tunnel they used for the Golden Hawk," he said to Scuffs. He left his laptop computer on the front seat of the Chevy and took the extra flashlight from the glove compartment. "Let's take a look."

"Worf?" said Scuffs.

"Don't be such a worrywart!" said Laptop. "What Grandpa Hotshoe doesn't know won't hurt him. Besides, they are all busy admiring the scenery. Let's go!"

The underground chamber that had seemed menacing and cold in the dark was now the most beautiful place Laura had ever seen. Stalactites hung from the ceilings in sheets of rippling stone, as fluid-looking as water—which was what had created them, after all.

It was like being inside a crystal held up to the sun. The roof was gold and light brown. Bats fluttered in and out among them, confused by the sudden, brilliant light.

The stream entered the cave from a low, dark

tunnel, and left through a bathtub-sized black hole. The water was only a foot deep, but very swift.

Laura bent down over the black hole. In the distance she could hear a mighty roar.

"This must be the sound we heard," she said. "I'll bet the stream leads to the waterfall."

Hotshoe and Annie weren't listening. They were busy trying out Wild Bill's cellular car phone.

It didn't work.

"Too much rock over our heads," said Hotshoe. "We'll have to go back outside to make a call. We had better hurry so we can meet the police when they arrive. Without our help, they may never find this place."

"That's the idea/the idea," said two voices in unison.

Hotshoe and Annie and Laura turned to see two sets of cold, menacing eyes.

A man and a woman, each dressed in silver spandex.

And each holding an Uzi machine gun.

MORE GAS!

Kin was having fun.

He was finally learning to drive. He loved the noise, the power, the speed—even though he wasn't going very fast.

It *felt* fast.

He even liked riding with a girl!

But Kin knew better than to pay attention to *that* feeling. He had seen enough TV to know that love caused nothing but trouble. He wasn't about to get a crush on Teresa and start acting stupid. No way!

Kin was immune to girls, no matter how—*interesting* they looked.

And certainly Teresa was interesting, with her ponytail and her violet eyes, even if they were phony as . . .

"You're not paying attention!"

"Huh?"

"I told you to slow down!" said Teresa. "This section of trail is pretty steep."

Kin slowed down. The trail led along the edge of a steep cliff.

"Think you can negotiate that?" Teresa asked.

"Sure," said Kin.

"Well, try it."

Kin gunned the ATV and he was off, following the narrow trail.

The rear wheels started to slip toward the edge.

Kin backed off on the throttle.

The wheels slipped even more.

"More gas," said Teresa. "More gas!"

Laptop led the way.

Scuffs followed faithfully.

This new tunnel was wide and straight—an exact twin of the tunnel that led in from the highway. Except that it led in the opposite direction, toward the other side of the mountain.

It grew darker and darker as they got farther and farther from the brightly lighted cavern.

Soon the only light was the dim beam of the flashlight.

Then the tunnel ended.

"Dead end?!" said Laptop. "I don't understand it. Unless . . ."

He reached out and touched the rock wall in front of him.

The rock moved under his hand.

"Worf!" said Scuffs.

"Papier-mâché!" exclaimed Laptop.

He pulled at the stone wall and it fell back out of the way.

Light poured in—brilliant, blinding light.

Squinting and covering his eyes, Laptop stepped forward into the light.

"Worf!" Scuffs pulled at his leg.

"Stop it!" said Laptop. "I can't believe you are biting me!"

He pushed the little dog away and took another step into the light.

"Worf worf!"

Scuffs jumped up and grabbed Laptop by the seat of his pants, and yanked him backwards with a growl.

And just in time!

Laptop blinked in amazement as his eyes adjusted to the light.

He was standing on a narrow ledge, only inches wide.

One more step and he would have fallen a thousand feet!

"Thanks, pal," he said to Scuffs. "You saved my hide for sure."

He knelt down to pat the little dog. As he bent over, he realized how narrow the ledge was.

Carefully, Laptop leaned over the edge and looked down.

His heart was pounding. An unfamiliar feeling of terror filled him from head to toe.

Laptop had never been afraid of heights before. He had even jumped three thousand feet to escape the air pirates who had been hijacking Wild Bill's car.

But this was different. From three thousand feet, the ground looked as far away and as soft as a dream.

From three hundred feet, it looked hard—and sharp—and deadly.

And he wasn't wearing a parachute!

"Worf," whined Scuffs.

"I know," said Laptop. "It's scary."

Below the ledge, a sheer cliff dropped hundreds of feet, into a nasty tangle of jagged boulders and splintered trees. The sharp rocks at the bottom of the cliff looked like the jaws of some giant beast, waiting to snap up whatever creature was unlucky enough to fall into its gaping maw!

Laptop wished there was something—anything! —on the ledge to hold onto. But there was nothing but smooth stone.

He looked up. Above, the cliff rose straight to the domelike top of Rockcastle Mountain.

To the right and the left, it was the same— sheer rock, straight up and down.

The tunnel behind the ledge where Laptop stood opened like a door in the center of the cliff under the top of Rockcastle Mountain.

"This is the spot where I thought the blimp crashed," Laptop said, looking up, then down. "The phony boulder hid the tunnel. The blimp must have swung the car into the entrance and then flew off."

The ledge was about a foot wide.

To the left, it narrowed to six inches, then

---

gave out altogether, blending into the sheer face of the cliff.

To the right, it disappeared around a smooth shoulder of rock.

Edging along carefully, one foot at a time, Laptop followed the ledge to the right, around the corner.

The ledge was slippery with gravel. Laptop knelt down and brushed it off. He didn't want to slip—one false step would be fatal!

He took another step, then another.

The further he went, the narrower the ledge got.

Above and below, it was the same—a vertical rock face, smooth except for a narrow network of cracks.

He had just rounded the rocky shoulder, when he heard a scraping sound behind him.

It sounded like it came from inside the tunnel.

"Did you hear that?" he whispered.

"Worf!" said Scuffs.

Laptop turned around and backtracked toward the tunnel entrance. He wanted to find out what had made the scraping noise.

But the tunnel entrance was gone!

Where the entrance had been, was a smooth "boulder" of gray papier-mâché. It had been rolled back into the entrance, sealing it tightly.

"Hey!" Laptop shouted. He banged on the papier-mâché "rock" with his fists.

He pulled on it. He tugged.

But nothing moved. It was sealed tight.

"Worf!" said Scuffs.

"You're telling me!" said Laptop. "Somebody has closed the entrance up behind us, and sealed it. We're trapped out here on this ledge!"

A GENETIC MASTERPIECE

"Better turn around," said Teresa.

"Aw!" Kin was disappointed.

He had managed to keep the ATV on the trail, just barely. The trail ahead was rough and steep, but he was sure he could make it. He had learned to shift smoothly, and to control the throttle.

All that was lacking was practice.

"This is not a good place to learn," said Teresa. "It's too steep by half. This trail leads all the way up to the top of the falls."

"Don't you want to see the top of the falls?" Kin ventured hopefully.

"Yeah," said Teresa, getting off. "So let me drive!"

"Aw!"

But Kin knew better than to argue. He was lucky to have gotten in as much practice as he had.

He slid to the back and Teresa got on in front.

"Put your arms around my waist," she said. "Go on, I won't bite."

Kin put his arms around her waist.

Teresa gunned the ATV and started up the trail, shifting expertly. Kin was amazed at how beautifully she handled the agile little machine. It was almost as if it were an extension of her own trim, athletic body.

The roar of the falls grew louder and louder. The spray was like a misty rain. The trail was slick, and the ATV's fat rear wheels kept slipping, but Teresa's hand on the throttle kept the machine under control.

"See how I steer with the throttle?" she said. "That's the key to racing success."

"I got you," said Kin, trying to concentrate. *I will not allow myself to get stupid!* he thought to himself. For the first time in his life, he was grateful to his little sister, Laura, for all the times she had hogged the TV remote control, making him watch idiotic romantic movies and soaps.

That was good training, Kin thought. *I have seen plenty of examples of how guys act when they fall in love, so I know all about how to avoid it. What if I didn't know anything about love? I would be a sitting duck for any girl, especially for a girl as pretty, and as bright, and as much fun as Teresa!*

"Look at those tracks!" Teresa said, and Kin snapped out of his reverie.

"Huh?"

Teresa slowed, pointing down at the muddy trail: deep paw prints.

"A big dog?" Kin ventured.

"Hah!" said Teresa. "You don't know the Smoky Mountains. That's bear."

"Bear!"

"Sure. There are lots of bears around here."

"Really?" Kin asked. "I thought bears were just in the olden days. I figured they were all in zoos by now."

"No way!" said Teresa. "In fact, they are making a comeback. Less land is used for farming, at least here in the East. And there are more bears than ever. Especially since the game conservation laws protect them."

"That's great," said Kin. "I guess."

"What do you mean, you guess? I love wildlife. The more the better."

"But, I mean, aren't bears dangerous?"

"It's people that are dangerous," said Teresa. "You never heard of a bear wiping out a forest, or polluting a river."

"You have a point there," said Kin. "Maybe I should learn more about wildlife and conservation."

"Maybe," said Teresa, grinning back over her shoulder.

Kin looked away. He didn't like looking into her violet eyes too much. It made his heart pound, and threatened to mess up his no-falling-in-love plan.

The *putuputuputup*-ing ATV wound through the trees. The trail was even muddier here, and the roar of the falls was even louder.

The ATV rounded the edge of a cliff, and looking up, Kin saw Sudden Falls, dropping hundreds of feet through the mist—dancing in the sun on rainbow feet.

"Beautiful, isn't it?" said Teresa.

"Yeah!" said Kin. Almost as beautiful as—

Just then something jumped out in front of the ATV.

Something little and furry.

Followed by something huge and hairy!

--- --- --- --- --- --- --- --- --- --- --- --- --- --- --- ---

"Greetings/greetings," said two voices in unison.

The man and woman in spandex held Hotshoe, Annie, and Laura at gunpoint.

They both wore nasty grins. As nasty as the guns they carried.

"What do you want?" demanded Hotshoe. *I wonder where Laptop is?* he thought to himself. *Maybe he's hiding. Maybe he'll be able to escape and get help. In the meantime, I'll keep these two busy.*

"Who are you and what do you want with us?"

"Want with you/with you? Nothing at all/at all," the two said in unison. "We intend to get rid of you/rid of you. But first, we need to dim the lights/dim the lights!"

Blam!

Blam!

The cave got darker as the man and woman in spandex shot out the headlights of the cars.

First the Ford Fairlane.

Blam!

Blam!

Then the Corvette.

"Stop!" said Hotshoe. "I'll turn the lights out if you want me to. But there's no point in destroying beautiful classic cars They're works of art!"

"That's why we want to ruin them/ruin them," said the man and woman in unison. "We hate beauty/beauty. We love evil/evil. You got a problem with that?"

"Sick!" said Annie.

"Disgusting," said Laura.

"Shut up, fools/fools!" said the man and woman in spandex. They spoke in unison, like a chorus. A mean, vicious, nasty little chorus of two.

"You should never have followed us here/ followed us here. Now you know too much/too much. You will pay for your nosiness/nosiness!" They waved their guns menacingly.

"Who are you?" asked Hotshoe.

"What do you want?" asked Infield Annie.

"And why do you talk in unison?" asked Laura.

"The last question is the only sensible question/ sensible question," said the man and woman in unison. "And the only one we will answer. We speak in unison because we are, in fact, one creature, a product of genetic engineering/genetic engineering. Our creator, Dr. Howard Howard, set out to design the perfect criminal/perfect criminal. We are the result: a genetic masterpiece/genetic masterpiece."

"You mean a genetic catastrophe," said Annie.

"Kindly keep your stupid opinions to yourself/to yourself," said the man/woman in unison. "Now hand over that antique you call a gun/you call a gun."

Reluctantly, Hotshoe handed the man his only weapon, the nineteenth-century Scottish black powder pistol.

The man handed it to the woman. She pulled back the hammer and took off the little brass percussion cap. She threw the cap into the darkness across the cave.

"Now it's useless/useless," he/she said in unison, as she tossed the pistol into the sand across the stream.

"We have already called the police," said Annie. "They are on their way."

"Yeah," said Hotshoe. "And one of us has already gone for help!"

"You mean the stupid kid with the ugly dog/ugly dog? He's stuck on a ledge outside/outside. That is, if he hasn't already fallen/already fallen.

"The police, those idiots, will never find this

cave/this cave. And for you we have a special surprise/special surprise."

The two waved their guns in unison. "This way/this way."

"We're in big trouble," muttered Hotshoe. "I hope Laptop isn't hurt."

"What creeps," whispered Annie.

"The spandex twins," whispered Laura.

The man and woman held the guns on Laura, Hotshoe, and Annie and walked them over to the black hole into which the stream disappeared.

"Behold your fate/your fate!" they said gleefully.

"A bear!" said Kin.

"A cub!" said Teresa.

The mama bear and baby bear stood in the center of the trail, looking confused.

Teresa threw the speeding ATV into a sharp power slide to miss the two bears.

Ka-whamp!

The ATV hit a tree, almost turned over, then righted itself and slid to a stop.

The cub ran off, sniffling in terror.

The mama bear looked at Kin and Teresa, shook her head—then followed her fleeing cub.

"Are you okay?" Kin asked.

"I think so," said Teresa.

"Is the ATV okay?"

"I think so. Yes. But we have a problem."

"Which is . . . ?"

"Look into my eyes," she said.

Kin did. They were green.

"Your eyes changed color!" said Kin. "Did we hit the tree that hard?"

"I lost my contacts, that's all," said Teresa, laughing. "But it means we have to turn back—because you have to drive."

Bam!

Bam!

"Did you hear that?" asked Laptop.

"Worf!"

"It sounded like gunshots! We have to get back into the tunnel."

Laptop pushed and pulled at the papier-mâché boulder. Even though it was soft, it was huge and heavy, and it sealed the entrance completely.

"It's no good," said Laptop. "We're stuck out here on this ledge. We'll have to get off this cliff and try to find another entrance."

But how?

The rock was smooth and straight up and down on all sides.

There was no way down.

No way up.

No way to the right.

But to the left . . . maybe!

"Come on," said Laptop.

With the little dog following, he edged slowly along the narrow ledge, around the smooth rock shoulder.

The ledge got narrower and narrower, and finally gave out altogether. But there was a narrow crack, leading up across the cliff at an angle.

Maybe if I use my toes, Laptop thought.

He started inching out onto the cliff face, leaning into the rock. For the first time, he was glad he had left his laptop computer in the cave.

"Worf."

Laptop looked back. Scuffs was still standing on the ledge.

Laptop inched back toward him.

"Well, come on, then," he said. "You'll have to ride on my back. Can you hold on?"

"Worf."

The little dog lay on Laptop's shoulders, with his paws crossed around his neck.

Kin started out again, inching along the crack. "Hold on," he said. "And don't look down!"

"Worf."

"Me neither."

INTO THE BLACK HOLE

"No way!" said Annie, outraged.

"I'm not going in there!" said Laura.

"I can't swim!" said Hotshoe.

"The question is, can you fly/can you fly?" asked the man and woman in unison, with two weird vicious grins.

They were holding Hotshoe, Annie, and Laura at gunpoint on the edge of the black hole with its swirling whirlpool.

"The water is shallow down in the hole/in the hole. It's fun, like a waterslide/waterslide," said the man and the woman in unison.

Doesn't look fun to me, thought Annie.

"You will be swept along for a few hundred yards, and then dumped into the main stream/main stream. Then you will emerge into

- - - - - - - - - - - - - - - - - -

the sunlight/into the sunlight . . . "

"Whew!" muttered Laura, feeling relief.

" . . . just before you are swept over the falls/over the falls."

"Oh, no you don't!" said Hotshoe.

He raised his fist and took a step toward the man and the woman.

They raised their guns. But instead of firing, they kicked in unison, like a pair of dancers.

Their heels caught Hotshoe in the chest. He spun backward and fell into the water.

"Hotshoe!" screamed Annie.

Hotshoe was swept around and around, down the black hole, into the darkness.

"Grandpa!" screamed Laura.

"I don't hear any more gunshots," said Laptop, as he inched his way up the cliff, with Scuffs clinging to his back. "Maybe Grandpa and Laura and Annie are okay."

"Worf."

"I kind of doubt it, too," said Laptop. "So let's hurry!"

Every time he looked down, Laptop felt a wave of vertigo. His heart pounded and his fingers started to tremble.

When Laptop was little, he had pretended that a dirt pile was a mountain so he could play mountain climber.

Now he pretended that a mountain was a dirt pile, so that he wouldn't get dizzy and fall.

He forced himself to concentrate on the rock at his fingertips and under his toes.

"Don't look down! Don't look down!" he muttered under his breath.

The crack got thinner and thinner, until Laptop's toes wouldn't fit into it.

He took off his sneakers and tied them together, then hung them around his neck.

"That's better," he said, jamming his toes into the crack.

Then it got too narrow for his toes.

"Lucky my toenails are long," he said, as he forced them into the tiny crack.

The crack led to another crack, and then another.

Higher and higher.

It was becoming easier and easier to hold on.

"Is it my imagination," said Laptop, "or is the cliff getting less steep?"

"Worf," said Scuffs.

- - - - - - - - - - - - - - - - -

"I believe you're right," said Laptop. "We're coming out on top!"

The cliff turned into a dome of rock, and soon Laptop was able to crawl on all fours, and then walk upright.

He set the dog down, and the two of them scrambled to the top of the mountain.

"Made it!"

On all sides, blue mountain ranges marched into the distance. It was beautiful—but Laptop had no time to enjoy the scenery.

He had to find a way to get back into the pirates' secret cavern.

"Worf! Worf!" said Scuffs, jumping in circles around a small bush that grew from a crack in the rock.

"Quit messing around!" Laptop said to the excited little dog. "We have to find the other entrance to the cave. Which means we have to go all the way back down to the road!"

"Worf!"

Impatiently, Laptop reached down to pick up the dog to carry him.

He felt a cool breeze on his fingertips.

"Whoa!" he said. "Is that what I think it is? Good dog, Scuffs. You found it!"

Cold cave air was blowing through a narrow crack in the dome.

Laptop lay down on the rock and stuck his head into the narrow crack.

He was in the cavern, looking down from the ceiling! Below, he could see several shadowy figures standing around the pool in the dim headlights of the cars.

Two of the figures had guns.

Laptop crawled in and pulled the dog after him—just in time to hear Laura scream:

"Grandpa!"

"It's them," whispered Laptop, looking down from the crack in the ceiling. "The two pirates who stole Wild Bill's Golden Hawk!"

"Worf," whispered Scuffs.

With the dog clinging to his neck again, Laptop slid silently and swiftly down a stalactite as if it were a fireman's pole.

At the bottom, he hid behind a stalagmite and tied on his sneakers.

The light in the cave was dim. It looked like the

pirates had shot out the headlights of all the cars but two—Wild Bill's Studebaker and Hotshoe's Chevy.

The two criminals in spandex held Laura and Annie at gunpoint. Laptop could hear them laughing and whispering in unison, cackling over their evil plans.

"I guess Grandpa's already a goner," said Laptop, choking back a tear. "They must have pushed him into the whirlpool. I have to find a way to save Laura. And Annie! I wish Kin was here."

"Worf," said Scuffs.

"Were here, then," said Laptop. "I don't see how you can worry about grammar at a time like this!"

Then Laptop saw Hotshoe's gun laying in the sand where the woman in spandex had tossed it.

"If I could only get to that gun without them seeing me!" he mused.

"Worf," whispered Scuffs.

"Huh?" Laptop looked down.

The little dog was gone.

"No!" yelled Laura.

From his hiding place, Laptop watched in horror as the two pirates pushed Laura and Annie toward the black whirlpool that had claimed Hotshoe.

He searched desperately for a rock, a stick—anything to throw!

Then he felt a familiar cold nose against his hand.

It was Scuffs—and he was carrying something!

"Good dog!" whispered Laptop, as he took the Scottish pistol from the little dog's mouth.

But too late, he thought to himself. His grandfather was already lost, swept into the tunnel.

Besides, the percussion cap was missing. The gun wouldn't fire without the cap.

Meanwhile, the two pirates were pushing Annie closer and closer to the black hole, getting ready to push her in.

"No!" Laura shouted, as they shoved Annie.

She fell into the black hole, and was gone.

"Two down/down," said the pirates in unison. "One more to go/go!"

"I hate you!" said Laura. "I hate you both!"

So do I, thought Laptop.

He weighed the heavy gun in his hand. If he threw it, he might hit one of them!

He stood up and took aim—

"Worf," said Scuffs.

The little dog was panting. Laptop saw something shiny on his tongue.

When did Scuffs get his tongue pierced? he wondered.

Then he realized—it was the brass cap!

"Good dog," he said, as he fitted it onto the gun under the hammer.

"No!" cried Laura as the pirates pushed her closer and closer to the black hole.

Only one shot, thought Laptop. *Which one?*

Then he looked up and saw the sheets of stalactites hanging down.

They might hit the pirates. They might hit Laura.

But he had no choice. They were backing his sister toward the black hole . . .

Laptop aimed at a cluster of stalactites right over the two pirates.

Baroom!

The old gun was three times as loud as the pirates' Uzis.

Smoke and echoing noise filled the cavern.

Ccrrraaaaaasssh!

There was a vast crashing sound, as stalactites fell in sheets, shattering on the floor all around.

When the smoke cleared, the two pirates were nowhere to be seen.

The cave was lighter than before.

But where was Laura?

There she was, leaning over the black hole. Covered with dust, but safe and sound.

And laughing!

"Why are you laughing?" Laptop asked angrily as he rushed to his sister's side. "Hotshoe and Annie were both lost down the black hole. That's nothing to laugh about!"

"Oh yeah?" said Laura. "Listen—"

Laptop heard a familiar voice from down in the hole: "Give us a hand, kids."

Amazed, he looked down.

Hotshoe and Annie were crawling out of the tunnel, wet and bedraggled, but smiling.

Laptop and Laura helped them up the steep, slick sides of the hole.

"What happened?" asked Laura. "I thought you were swept over the falls for sure."

"We almost were," said Hotshoe. "The water in

that tunnel is terribly swift! But those two pirates didn't take my belt. I was able to make a loop and lasso a stalagmite—those are the ones that stick up. Then I grabbed Annie as she went by."

"We could hear the falls just ahead," said Annie. "It was scary."

"Where are the pirates?" asked Hotshoe, looking around in amazement. "What happened here?"

A door-sized hole had been opened in the ceiling of the cavern. The floor of the cave was littered with broken stalactites, all of which had miraculously missed the cars.

"One shot from your black powder pistol brought it all down," said Laptop. "It must have been the tremendous noise. The pirates may be buried under the stalagmites—"

"Stalactites," corrected Hotshoe.

"Whatever. Or they could have gotten away."

Bbbrrroom!

Bbbrrroom!

Two motorcycles were heard starting in the distance.

"There's your answer," said Annie. "Their motorcycles must have been hidden in the tunnel. They're getting away!"

"Maybe my computer's cellular modem will work now," said Laptop, looking up at the hole in the ceiling. "We can alert the police to be looking for them!"

"Worf," said Scuffs.

Laptop ran to Hotshoe's 1955 Chevy, where he had left his trusty Apricot 07. On his way back, he jumped the stream, but his foot slipped when he landed, and he dropped the computer—into the water.

"Oh, no!" Laura cried.

"Don't worry," said Laptop. "It's the waterproof diver's model. It even floats."

"The problem is, it's floating toward the black hole!" said Hotshoe.

He tried to snag it with his belt, but missed.

"Worf!" said Scuffs.

The courageous little dog jumped into the narrow stream and dog-paddled toward the floating computer.

He grabbed it in his jaws and started paddling against the current.

"Come on, Scuffs!" shouted Laura.

"Good dog," said Annie.

But the swift current was carrying the dog

toward the black hole. As Annie, Laptop, and Hotshoe watched in horror, the whirlpool sucked Scuffs in and spun him around and around.

"I'm coming!" Laptop cried. With Annie holding his hand, he leaned down into the black hole.

"Got you!" he cried.

But all he had was the computer.

"Worf! Woooooooorrrrf!" cried Scuffs as the current spun him around and around, faster and faster—

Down the hole.

Into the darkness.

Gone.

JUST A DOG

Beep beep beep.

"What's that beeping noise?" Kin asked.

"Got me," said Teresa.

"Well, I wish we could turn it off. It's ruining my concentration."

Kin was concentrating on easing the ATV slowly down the steep, narrow trail.

Under the wheels, the rock was wet and slick with spray from the falls. On one side was a sheer rock wall; on the other, a cliff dropped off a hundred feet.

It was all Kin could do to keep the ATV from sliding off. But without her contacts, Teresa was helpless. He had to drive!

Up above on the rocks, he could see the bear chasing her frightened cub. At least they were safe.

"Shift down to low," said Teresa. "You need engine braking to slow you down."

"Okay," said Kin.

Beep beep beep.

"There it is again," said Teresa. "It's the radio."

"What radio?"

"There's a two-way, here on the ATV. Under the tank."

"Well, you answer it," said Kin. "I need both hands just to stay on the trail."

"I'm getting a lot of static," said Teresa. "It sounds like your little brother. He says they are in a cave at the top of the mountain."

"What a time to go spelunking," muttered Kin.

"There's something about the dog."

"What?" asked Kin as he maneuvered slowly around a steep curve.

"There's a lot of static. The dog . . . in the stream. The waterfall . . ."

"What!?"

"Something about help . . ."

Kin looked up. The trail switchbacked all the way up the cliff to the top of the falls. It made him dizzy just to look at it.

He jammed on the brakes.

"What are you doing?" Teresa asked.

"Turning around," said Kin, gunning the ATV. "We're going up the trail to the top of the falls!"

"But . . . but . . ."

"It's no use," said Laptop. "Even with the hole in the ceiling, I can't get hold of anybody. At least, nobody is responding."

"Can we go after him?" Laura asked, leaning over to peer down into the black hole.

"Get back, honey!" said Annie.

"It's no use," said Hotshoe. "The current is too swift down there. He's already halfway to the falls."

"Let's head for the highway, then," said Laura, who was surprised to realize how much she loved the faithful little dog. "Maybe if we drive real fast to the Sudden Falls overlook . . ."

"It'll be too late," said Laptop despondently.

"It's all we can do!" said Hotshoe. "Come on! We'll come back for the cars later."

Hotshoe, Laura, and Annie took off running, into the tunnel that led back to the highway.

Laptop was just about to follow them when he heard a familiar sound, above and behind him.

Whomp!
Whomp!
Whomp!

He looked up and saw the state police helicopter, hovering over the hole in the ceiling. Wild Bill was leaning out and dropping a rope ladder down into the cavern.

"You all go ahead!" Laptop shouted down the tunnel. "I'll meet you at the falls."

And he ran for the rope ladder.

"Are you sure you can do this?" asked Teresa as the ATV roared up the switchbacks.

"I'm sure," said Kin. "I think."

"Stay in second," said Teresa. "Use your power. It's the only thing that'll keep you pointed the way you want to go."

The ATV's fat rear wheels slipped and slid on the steep, narrow trail.

On the turns, the rear tires hung out over empty space.

Kin tried looking down—once.

It made him dizzy, so he concentrated on the trail racing by under the front wheels.

The spray was as heavy as rain at first. Then it

got lighter as the ATV clawed its way higher and higher.

The trail ran across bare rock. The rear wheels started to slip down the slope.

Kin slowed down.

"More gas!" screamed Teresa. "If you slow down, we'll slide off!"

Kin twisted the throttle, and the ATV leaped forward. Far above, he could see the bear, running lightly across the rocks, still chasing its terrified cub.

"I can't believe we're doing this," said Teresa. "He's just a dog."

"Just a dog!?!" Kin protested. "Scuffs is family! We can't abandon him in his time of need."

"He's still just a dog," Teresa muttered to herself.

TOWARD THE EDGE

Rock. Water. Air.

Rock. Water. Air.

Over and over . . .

Tumbling through the darkness, Scuffs would have known what a dime feels like, left in a pair of jeans in the washing machine.

Except that Scuffs didn't know what a dime was.

Or a pair of jeans.

Or a washing machine.

All he knew was that he was tumbling faster and faster, through a darkness of

Rock.

Water.

Air.

Over and over . . .

• • • • •

"Hurry!" cried Laptop as Wild Bill pulled him into the hovering helicopter.

"Is that my Studebaker Golden Hawk I see down there?" Wild Bill asked.

"Yes, and it's safe," said Laptop. "But Scuffs isn't."

"Scuffs?"

"My dog. He's being swept over the falls. Hurry! Maybe we can save him!"

"We can try," said Trooper Thom, who was at the controls of the sleek state police chopper.

He swooped low over the mountaintop, toward the rocky cleft where the stream rushed out of the cavern.

Laptop could see the town of Sudden Falls far below. He could see the highway where Hotshoe's RV and Annie's VW were parked. Directly below the helicopter, the water rushed out of the mountain and then disappeared in a thousand-foot plunge.

"See him?" asked Trooper Thom, throttling down toward the parking lot by the top of the falls.

"Not yet," said Laptop. "We may be too early."

Or too late, he thought silently.

On the far side of the falls, a trail switchbacked up from the valley floor.

A bright yellow and blue ATV was racing up the steep, narrow trail.

"Wow," said Trooper Thom. "That driver is sure slapping leather!"

"That dude is race ready!" said Wild Bill admiringly.

"That's my brother!" shouted Laptop. "And look—"

With his nose pressed against the Plexiglass dome of the copter, he pointed down toward the rushing stream.

A little yellow speck was dog-paddling fiercely, being swept inexorably toward the falls.

"There's my dog!" Laptop cried. "Scuffs!"

"He's too far away," said Trooper Thom. "We'll never get to him in time."

"Good riding," said Teresa as the ATV soared over the last rise of the trail, the wheels barely touching the ground. "Now shift up."

Kin clutched and kicked the gearshift up into third.

The front wheels reared up as the ATV roared forward, across the wide parking lot toward the overlook, where the stream went over the falls.

"I see him!" Kin cried. "Scuffs! Scuffs!"

"Worf," answered the desperate little dog.

Kin screeched to a stop, and leapt off the ATV. "Wait here!" he cried out to Teresa as he jumped the fence and ran down the rocks toward the stream.

Whomp.

Whomp.

Whomp.

As he ran he looked up and saw a state police helicopter hovering over the water. But it was too high, and Kin saw that the rescue was up to him.

The brave little dog was getting closer and closer to the edge. There was no way to reach him. No time . . .

"Worf!" cried Scuffs as he was swept toward the falls.

Just then a hairy arm reached out of the rocks and grabbed the waterlogged dog by the scruff of his neck.

Could it be? Kin wondered.

It was!

The bear.

"Worf," said Scuffs as he was lifted out of the icy rushing water.

He was looking into huge brown eyes.

They looked disappointed.

The bear tossed him aside.

"Ooof!" Scuffs grunted as he hit the rocky bank.

He stood up and shook the water off his fur.

"Worf," he said in thanks. But the big black bear that had saved him was already disappearing into the brush.

.A helicopter landed in the parking lot. Now an RV and a VW were pulling in, too.

Three familiar figures were running down the rocks toward the stream. Scuffs ran up to meet them.

"Worf! Worf! Worf!"

Laptop, Kin, and Laura.

"Did you see that?" Laptop asked.

"Did I ever," said Kin.

"Thanks!" called out Laura.

"Yeah!" said Laptop. "Thanks a lot!"

"Grrrmmpphh," said the bear as she disappeared into the laurel thickets.

"Don't bother thanking her," said Kin as he picked up Scuffs. "She wasn't trying to help us. She was just looking for her lost cub."

WHERE'S THAT GIRL?

"Where is that girl?" asked Hollis Wabash III.

It was getting late.

It was almost show time.

The Sudden Falls High School gym was filling up with race drivers, mechanics, pit crews, helpers, fans, and just plain folks eager to hear an evening of country music.

Von, the leader, was tuning his guitar.

Gar, the bass player, was adjusting the amplifiers.

Hal, on keyboards, was setting up his stand.

Rue, the drummer, was attaching cymbals to his complicated trap set.

Hollis Wabash III was sitting with Waddy and Bill Elliott at a table near the front of the gym. With them was Infield Annie.

The gym was buzzing with anticipation. Everyone was ready to have fun.

But where was the main act?

"Where is that girl?" asked Hollis Wabash III again, checking his Rolex.

"She'll be along," said Annie. "I left her at the top of the mountain with her grandpa and her two brothers. They had to show the police where to find the stolen cars, and then they were going to come right down."

"She should have left early and come with you," said Hollis.

"You know how young folks are," said Annie. "After all the excitement, she wanted to be with her family for a while. She'll be along."

"And what about my daughter?" Waddy asked.

"She's with Kin," Annie said with a smile. "They seem sort of attached to each other. They'll be along with the others."

"You all hush up," said Bill Elliott. "The show is starting. I want to hear the Beach Boys."

"Beach Dudes," said Hollis.

"These aren't the Beach Boys?" asked Bill and Waddy. They both sounded disappointed.

● ● ● ● ●

They soon got over their disappointment.

The Beach Dudes played a wild and crazy set that had the whole gym dancing and cheering.

"Where is that girl!" Hollis muttered as the last song ended. He checked his Rolex again.

"That sure is a noisy watch," said Annie.

"Huh?" Hollis put the watch to his ear. "That's not my watch."

Whomp.

Whomp.

Whomp.

"That sound is coming from outside," he said.

Soon there was a crowd on the front steps of the gym, watching the helicopter land.

Out stepped the star of the show—Laura Travis.

Hollis Wabash III ran under the whirling rotor and helped her out of the helicopter.

"I was getting worried," he said. "The Beach Dudes played a great set, but the crowd is getting ready for some real country music."

"I hope I can give them what they want," said Laura. "But I have to wait for my guitar. It's on its way in Hotshoe's RV."

She went into the gym to listen while the Beach Dudes played an encore. In between surfin' songs, she told "Awesome Bill" and Hollis and Waddy about the day's adventures.

"Wild Bill and Trooper Thom are up there clearing out the classic cars," she said. "The pirates got away—again! Teresa and Kin are riding down with Hotshoe, and so are Laptop and Scuffs."

"And, now," said Von, the leader of the Beach Dudes, "here's the evening's star attraction—"

"That's your cue," said Waddy.

"But I don't have my guitar!" protested Laura.

"That's not a problem," said Hollis Wabash III. He reached under the table and pulled out a brand new Wabash Cannonball guitar.

"It's beautiful!" Laura said. "I can hardly wait to play it!"

"Go, then," said Hollis, giving her a little push up onto the stage.

Von took Laura's hand and whispered, "What do you want us to call you? Just Laura, or Laura Travis?"

"I have a better idea," Laura said, remembering the day's adventures in the high laurel thickets around the top of Rockcastle Mountain.

110

She whispered in Von's ear, and he smiled. "Great idea," he whispered back.

Then he spoke into the mike.

"And, now, to continue our show honoring NASCAR families, here is the newest flower of country music—

"Mountain Laurel!"

"I hope we're in time," said Kin as Hotshoe's RV pulled up in front of the gym.

He and Teresa got out, followed by Laptop and Hotshoe, and of course, Scuffs. The ATV had been left at the top of the mountain, to be brought down on the trailer with the rescued classic cars.

They all ran for the gym.

"We made it!" said Kin as he slipped in the front door.

"Great!" whispered Teresa, sliding in behind him.

There on the stage was Laura, standing in the spotlight singing.

But something was wrong.

She was awful!

MAY I HAVE THIS DANCE?

As soon as she struck her first chord, Laura knew something was wrong.

She couldn't remember the words.

She couldn't remember the notes.

Couldn't sing. Couldn't play.

It was a nightmare. She was standing in front of hundreds of people, on a brightly lighted stage, holding a guitar she didn't know what to do with!

After the first few awkward notes, Von and the Beach Dudes came to the rescue.

They kicked in behind her, playing a fast instrumental, as if it had been planned all along.

As soon as everyone was dancing, Laura ran off the stage in tears.

"What happened?" asked Kin, who rushed backstage with Hotshoe, Annie, and Laptop to meet her.

"I thought you could play and sing."

"I thought I could, too!" said Laura. "But I can't!"

"Oh, honey!" said Hotshoe. "It's okay."

"I guess you're not ready for prime time," said Hollis Wabash III, looking very grim.

"I know what the problem is!" said Laptop.

He ran out to Hotshoe's RV.

He ran back in, carrying the old guitar that had belonged to Laura's mother. "Try this one," he said. "The one Annie gave you."

"Foolishness," said Hollis Wabash III.

"Worth a try," said Annie and Kin.

"Oh, honey!" said Hotshoe.

Laura picked up the guitar. She looked doubtful.

The Beach Dudes finished the instrumental to wild applause. Kin looked at Hollis, and Hollis shrugged.

Kin pushed Laura back onto the stage.

"One more try," he called after her.

Von, who had been watching all this, took her hand and led her to the mike.

"And now another song from our newest star, Mountain Laurel . . ."

He sounded a little uncertain. But his uncertainty turned to smiles as soon as Laura hit the first note of "Stand By Your Man."

The gym was filled with music.

Laura—Mountain Laurel—smiled as she sang. She knew the words.

She knew the notes.

Her fingers flew across the strings.

The nightmare had turned into a dream!

For her third number, Laura sang "Your Cheatin' Heart," and everyone got up to dance. The first real slow dance.

Teresa tapped Kin on the shoulder. "Remember me? Want to dance?"

"I, uh—" stammered Kin.

Dancing with her was the last thing he wanted to do. What if he fell in love? Then he would get stupid for sure!

But Teresa was already dragging him onto the floor.

"You'll have to lead," she said. "I'm blind as a bat without my contacts."

She snuggled into his arms.

Kin relaxed. *It's just for one dance,* he

NASCAR • RACE READY

thought, *And I've already proved that I can resist falling in love. Though her green eyes are even prettier without the contacts* . . .

After a slow song or two, Mountain Laurel played a fast-paced breakdown, "Billy in the Low Ground." The Beach Dudes backed her up. Hal, the keyboard player, doubled on the fiddle, his dreadlocks swinging.

Laura found herself picking a complex guitar lead! Her fingers knew exactly what to do.

Soon the whole room was dancing. One group formed a circle, clapping and laughing as they danced.

Laura was astonished when she saw why they were laughing.

In the middle of the circle a bear cub was dancing awkwardly.

Could it be? she wondered.

It was. The dancers' delight turned to panic as the door opened, and a huge, dark, hairy shape appeared in the doorway.

The mama bear!

The crowd parted like the Red Sea. The bear growled and the cub ran into her arms. She growled again and shambled off into the night, slamming the door behind her.

"Mother love," said Bill Elliott to Waddy.

"I hope she's happy now," said Hotshoe.

"Worf," said Scuffs as the band struck up another number.

(UN)FINISHED BUSINESS

The concert was over.

It had been a big success.

"Goodnight," said Teresa.

"Goodnight," said Annie.

"Goodnight," said Waddy and Bill Elliott and Steve Gregson, and the crowd of NASCAR drivers and workers and wives. Goodnight, goodnight, goodnight . . .

The big gym was almost empty.

Laura and Kin and Laptop were on stage, helping the Beach Dudes put away their amps and instruments.

"You guys were great," said Laura. "Thanks for helping me out."

"If you ever need a regular backup band, let us know," said Von.

"For sure," agreed Gar, Hal, and Rue.

Laptop and Scuffs helped the "dudes" carry their instruments out to their Pontiac hearse.

"What's with you and Teresa?" Laura asked Kin when they were alone on the empty stage.

"What do you mean?" asked Kin.

"You know what I mean."

"That's ridiculous," said Kin, reddening.

"Then why are you blushing?"

"I'm not blushing. And I've got better things to do than get a crush on some girl and start acting stupid, like they do in the movies!"

"Okay, okay!" said Laura.

"I'm immune to love!" said Kin.

"Sure," said Laura. "I believe you."

You do? Kin wondered.

"Excuse me?"

They both turned.

A shadowy figure had just entered the empty gym.

"Don't you people ever return your calls?"

It was a woman. She walked toward the stage, into the light.

Kin and Laura stared, amazed.

"Aunt Adrian!"

More later . . .

About the Author

T. B. Calhoun is the pseudonym of an experienced mechanic who has written on automotive topics as well as penned award-winning science fiction and fantasy novels. Like Darrell Waltrip, Jeremy Mayfield, and other NASCAR stars, Calhoun is a native of Owensboro, Kentucky. He currently resides in New York City.

BE A NASCAR WINNER...
With this exciting NASCAR Sweepstakes!

One lucky Grand Prize Winner, along with their parent
or legal guardian, will receive a FREE trip to the official
NASCAR SpeedPark™ in Myrtle Beach, SC
Fifty Second Prize Winners will receive a NASCAR SpeedPark T-shirt.

TO ENTER:

Send in contest entry form located at the back
of NASCAR Rolling Thunder, NASCAR Race Ready,
and NASCAR In The Groove **OR** send a 3 x 5 card
complete with your name, address, telephone
number and birthday to the address below:

ENTER THE NASCAR SWEEPSTAKES

Mail this entry form along with
the following information to:

**HarperCollins Publishers
10 East 53rd Street
New York, NY 10022
Attn: Department AW**

Name:

Address:

City: State: Zip:

Phone #: Birthday: / /